This book belongs to:

_____

Kit

MAYA

Prakash

WINNIE

Sam & Tom

Little Acorns
NURSERY

EMILY

Rex

HONEY

George

SOPHIE

For all the mini foodies and fussy eaters - F.C

For Harry - S.D

This paperback edition first published in 2020 by Andersen Press Ltd.
First published in Great Britain in 2018 by Andersen Press Ltd.,
20 Vauxhall Bridge Road, London SW1V 2SA.

Printed and bound in China.
1 3 5 7 9 10 8 6 4 2
British Library Cataloguing in Publication Data available.
ISBN 978 1 78344 758 9

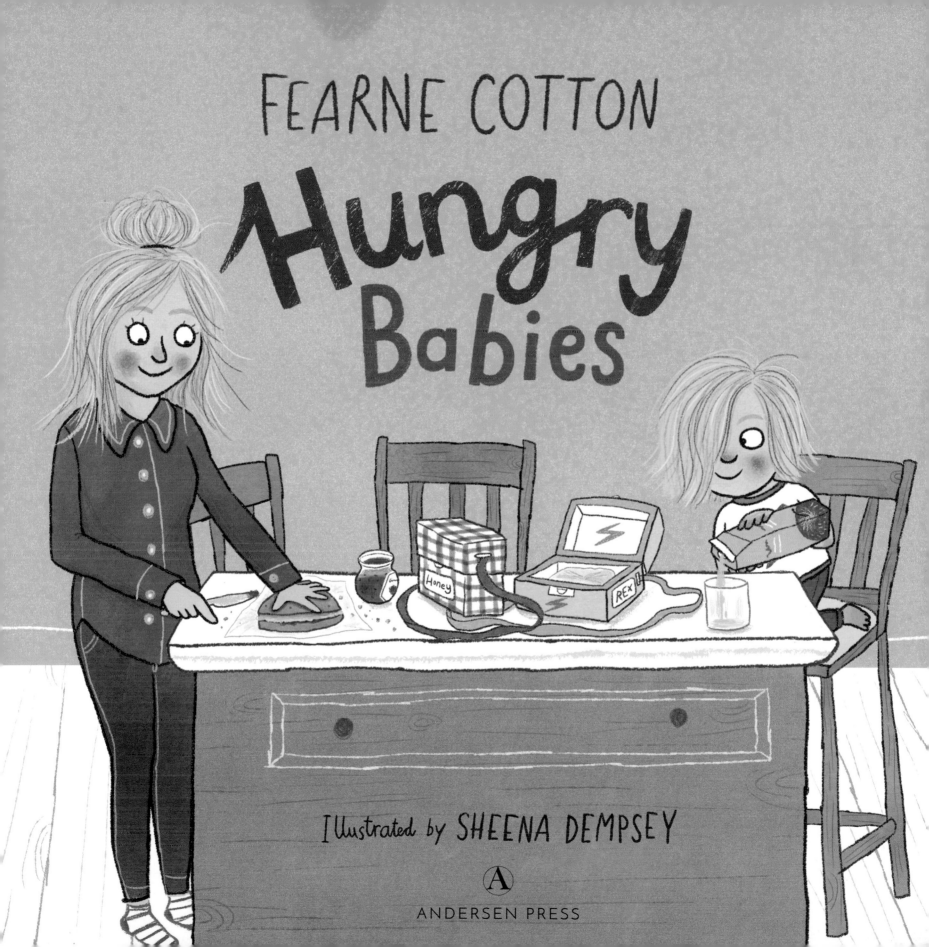

We're the Hungry Babies,
look what we can eat:
fruit and veg, milk and bread,
sometimes a little treat.

Rex eats toast for breakfast.
Today he wants to share –
Bingo can't believe his luck,
what a naughty pair!

Honey likes to feed herself.
Oh dear, what a mess!
Food on her face and in her hair,
and down her pretty dress.

Poor Emily's unwell today,
wants cuddles from her mum.
No nursery or food for her –
she's got a poorly tum.

Prakash is at the market,
helping Granny shop:
fresh fruit in the basket
and mango down his top.

We're the Hungry Babies
waiting for our lunch.
Kit likes to eat bananas –
"Don't eat that whole bunch!"

Sophie loves a picnic,
her lunch spread on a rug.
Sandwiches and strawberries,
and juice drunk from a mug.

Today is Maya's birthday.
She's going out to eat.

Please
WAIT
to be
SEATED

But Jack is so annoying,
and won't stay in his seat.

He runs around the restaurant,
makes bubbles with his straw,

hits Maya with his menu,
spills juice all on the floor!

Then the fish and chips arrive
and Jack eats all his food.
Maya's birthday treat is fun
(but that burp from Jack was rude).

George likes cheese on everything:
his pasta and his bread,
his yogurt and his jelly,
and sometimes on his head!

Winnie's in the kitchen,
helping Daddy bake:
sausage rolls for teatime
and a giant chocolate cake.

We're the Hungry Babies.
"Snack time now," says Mum.
"Yuk!" says Tom. "Don't like it."
Sam says, "Yummy yum."

It's birthday tea at Maya's house,
all her friends have come.
There's lots of food for everyone
and leftovers for Mum.

Yes we're the Hungry Babies,
from morning through to night.
With milk to drink at bedtime
as we cuddle up so tight.

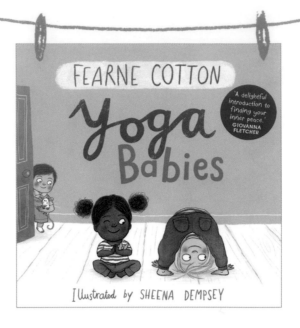

'A delightful introduction to finding your inner peace.'
Giovanna Fletcher

'Follow these chilled-out tots practising their yoga moves
everywhere, from the garden to bedtime.'
Mail on Sunday

'Sheena Dempsey's artwork makes this sweet picture book featuring young
children doing different yoga poses come alive... if there's a yoga-loving mum
or dad in the family, this is the perfect book for the whole household.'
Irish Independent, Best Books of 2017

'Sweet story... read it together and you can act out the moves!'
Mother & Baby